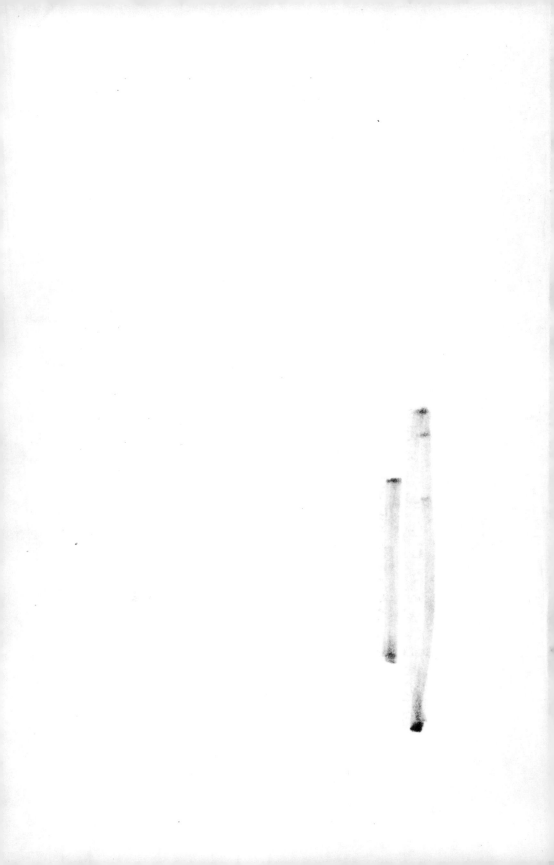

The Heart of Cool

The HEART of COOL

BY JAMIE MᶜEWAN
PICTURES BY
SANDRA BOYNTON

Ready-to-Read
Simon & Schuster Books for Young Readers
New York   London   Toronto   Sydney   Singapore

First Simon & Schuster Books for Young Readers edition May 2001

Simon & Schuster Books for Young Readers
An imprint of Simon & Schuster Children's Publishing Division
1230 Avenue of the Americas
New York, New York 10020

Book design by Sandra Boynton

Printed and bound in the United States of America
2 4 6 8 10 9 7 5 3 1

Library of Congress Cataloging-in-Publication Data
McEwan, James.
The heart of cool / by James McEwan; illustrated by Sandra Boynton.
p.   cm. — (Ready-to-read)
Summary: When Bobby moves to a new school, he tries to be the
ultimate in cool by imitating Harry Haller, the coolest kid of all.
ISBN 0-689-82177-8 (hc.)
[1. Schools—Fiction. 2. Self-acceptance—Fiction.] I. Boynton, Sandra, ill.
II. Title. III. Series.
PZ7.M478463Hg   1999
[E]—dc21   98-36614
CIP   AC

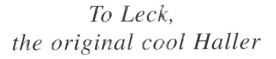

To Leck,
the original cool Haller

Contents

New Bear on the Block

When Bobby North came to his new school, he found that he was the smallest guy in his class.

He found that action figures were not cool.

He found that white coats were completely not cool.

"Okay," he said, "so what *is* cool?"

"I'm cool," said Siggy Sidewinder.

"Yeah, you're pretty cool," said Derek Mack. "But how about Harry Haller?"

"Harry's *ultra* cool," admitted Siggy.

CHAPTER ONE

The Emperor of Cool

Everybody agreed: Harry Haller was the coolest kid in the school, maybe the world.

Harry was never scared, or worried, or embarrassed. He always knew the right thing to say, and whatever happened, he always knew the right thing to do. Harry was the Emperor of Cool.

Harry could do
unbelievable stunts
on his skateboard.

And if he fell down,
he just bounced up again
with a laugh.

Even the teachers thought Harry was cool. "Yo, Mr. Castor. What's up?" Harry would ask the school principal with a wave of his hand, and Mr. Castor would smile and wave back. Nobody else dared to ask Mr. Castor "What's up?"

Bobby wanted to be just like Harry Haller.

When Bobby had the chance, he would follow Harry around and listen to everything he said and watch everything he did. At night Bobby went home and practiced being like Harry in front of the mirror.

Bobby saved up to buy the right scarf and sunglasses.

Bobby traded his action figures for a used skateboard. On weekends and after school he rode it for hours, trying all the most radical moves.

"Hey, look who's the hot rider now!" Siggy said, laughing.

Bobby kept trying.

After a while he stopped falling off his skateboard.

He learned some good riffs on his harmonica.

He scored a goal in Saturday soccer.

And it worked. "Come on, Bobby," said Derek in the lunch line one day. "Sit with us, dude."

Bobby had made it. Now everybody said he was cool.

Well—almost everybody.

CHAPTER TWO

Way Cool

But Bobby wasn't satisfied. He didn't want people to just *think* he was cool. He wanted to *be* truly cool, totally cool, cool all the way down to the core.

So he read cool books.

He watched cool movies with cool stars.

He ate cool, he slept cool, he walked cool, and he talked cool.

He even sat in his room and thought cool thoughts.

One spring day when the bell rang at the end of math class, Bobby didn't get out of his seat.

"Come on, let's go to recess, Bobby," said Frannie Woggle.

Bobby didn't move.

"Look, guys! Bobby fell asleep in class," said Siggy.

"But his eyes are open," said Derek. "What's the matter, Bobby?"

Bobby didn't answer.

"Hey, Mr. Quirk!" called Lily Root. "Something's wrong with Bobby."

Mr. Quirk had a thorough look at Bobby and called in the school nurse.

Nurse Shikes had a very thorough look at Bobby and called the doctor.

Dr. Bock had an extremely thorough
look at Bobby. "I don't see anything
wrong with him," said the doctor,
"except that he's a little chilled. Has he
been outside recently?"

"No, he's been in a warm classroom," Mr. Quirk told her.

The doctor sighed. "Just to be on the safe side," she said, "we'd better call an ambulance."

"Whoa, hold on a second," said a voice from the doorway. In strolled Harry Haller. Everybody stood back while Harry stared into Bobby's eyes.

"Nothing's wrong with him," said
Harry. He clapped Bobby on the
shoulder. "Congratulations, Bobby,
you did it, you're there, you've arrived."
Bobby didn't answer, but a small smile
crept onto his face.

Harry spoke a little louder. "Okay now, you've got to warm up a little, just enough to get you to recess. You can find it again anytime, no problem."

Bobby turned his head and blinked. "Wow. I really did it, didn't I, Harry? I was *there*."

"Oh, totally, man, ab-so-lute-ly, right at the center, right at the heart of cool. Come on, I've got your books."

CHAPTER THREE

Siggy Doubts

For a while Bobby was the coolest guy in his class. Harry called him "my main man" and invited him to practice with his rock group, Harry and the Flame-Tops.

Bobby practiced with them, but he never dyed his hair.

Some of the smaller kids started following him around to try and learn how to walk the way he did. But Bobby soon stopped doing his cool walk.

He only wore his sunglasses when it was sunny.

He only wore his scarf when it was cold.

He didn't have to *try* to be cool. He already was cool. He'd been there. Right at the heart of it.

But one day Siggy Sidewinder came
up to him and said, "Hey, you know,
Bobby, I don't think you're really very
cool at all."

"Okay," Bobby said, then turned
back to his friends.

"Okay *what*?" Siggy asked loudly.

"Okay, you
don't think I'm
cool," Bobby said.

"But if you're not cool, then what was all that stuff about you being so chilled-out you couldn't move? Cool trance, *HA!* You were just faking it!"

"I wasn't faking it."

"Then prove it!" Siggy yelled. "Prove it, if you're so cool! Come to Harry's on Friday night. Harry's dad just finished a new half-pipe in his backyard. Harry's having a party, with a big contest. Come strut your stuff and show us your best cool tricks. We'll see how cool you are."

"I'm not much into tricks these days," said Bobby.

"I saw you skateboarding at the park," Siggy said.

"I still board," replied Bobby.

"So the real story," said Siggy, "is that you're just too much of a wimp to show us what you've got. Friday night—at six o'clock. If you're not there, man, you will be forever and totally uncool."

Bobby watched Siggy walk away.

"You going to go?" Derek asked him.

"I'd like to go," said Bobby. Then he frowned. "But I'm not sure I want to be in a contest. Especially not a How-Cool-Are-You? contest."

"You can't just let Siggy win," said Obediah.

Bobby looked at Derek. He looked at Frannie, Lily, and Obediah. They looked back at him, waiting for an answer.

"Wait a minute," said Bobby, "are you telling me that if Siggy rides better than I do, you'll think he's cool? And that I'm *not* cool?"

At first, nobody answered. Then Lily spoke up: "No, but you should go. Go give it a try. Not giving it a try is not cool."

"Yeah, I want to see it," said Derek.

Bobby thought about it. He did want to try out the new half-pipe.

"Okay," Bobby said, "I'll go. But I don't know about doing tricks."

CHAPTER FOUR
Air Time

Bobby was there on Friday. But most
of the time he was lost in the crowd.
He watched as the smaller kids tried out
Harry's half-pipe. They were having a lot
of fun.

Then the contest started. Bobby watched the bigger kids show off their best tricks. Derek did some cool grinds and board slides. Frannie dropped in from the platform and caught air on the far side.

"Come on, Harry, your turn!" Kids started to shout.

"No, no," said Harry. "I'm not skating tonight. It wouldn't be fair; this thing lives in my backyard. How about Siggy?"

Siggy had been waiting. He dropped in like a shot and put on a real show— rock-and-rolls, reverts and inverts, hand-plants and twists. Everybody shouted and cheered. They were sure Siggy would win.

When Siggy was finished, he called to Bobby. "Okay, big man, your turn! Show us how Mr. Totally Cool does it."

"Hey, I never said I was Mr. Cool." Bobby climbed up to the platform with his board while some kids cheered and some hooted below him.

Bobby had spent every afternoon that week practicing in the park. He was boarding pretty well. He knew he could still make all the moves.

But being cool wasn't all tricks, was it?

As he stood up there, the crowd got really quiet—and Bobby felt nervous. His knees started to shake. *Oh, no*, he thought. *I've got to find cool.*

He closed his eyes. It was there, somewhere. He knew he could find it . . .

Bobby heard the kids start to whistle
impatiently. He heard cars passing on
the road and a dog barking far away.
He looked up and saw the moon and
the stars,
thousands of stars.

Bobby dropped down the steep ramp.

The plywood rumbled as he shot across the flat, up the far side, and up into the air. He slapped one hand on the deck, turned, and tore across to catch air on the far side. The next time across he kicked off with his foot and got higher still.

"Bo-ring! Bo-ring!" Siggy started shouting, and soon half the crowd was chanting along with him: "Bor-ing! Bor-ing! Bor-ing!"

Bobby hardly noticed. He got higher and higher. This was fun. It felt so good just to get up into the air. He almost felt as if he could take off, right up into the night sky, up with the moon and the planets.

Then, one time, he didn't turn back. He launched himself up and didn't turn. He flew up and up, right over the railing, out of the light, and into the darkness.

A hush fell over the crowd as Bobby
seemed to hover up there, a vague shape
against the stars. It looked as if he were
truly flying.

Then he was gone.

Crash!

Everyone came running. Bobby
crawled out through a gap in the hedge.
"Wow, cool…" said Bobby, still
looking up at the night sky. "But where
did this hedge come from?"

CHAPTER FIVE

Soft Landing

At lunch on Monday, almost no one sat at Bobby's table. Siggy came up, wearing the hat he'd won Friday night, with a whole crowd behind him. "Yo, Bobby," he shouted, "checked out any cool bushes recently?" Then he laughed. "Look, guys! Look at all those great bandages and that neat-o sling!"

The whole crowd laughed with him. But then Harry came up beside them, and they got quiet really fast.

Harry just stood there for a minute, looking at Bobby. Kids all around stopped talking to watch. Soon Bobby was the only one in the room who was still eating.

Finally Bobby looked up.

"Tell me, Bobby," said Harry. Everybody in the lunchroom leaned forward to hear. Even the servers behind the counter stopped serving to listen. "What about that stunt you pulled Friday night? Was it cosmically cool, or incredibly uncool? You should be able to tell us, 'cause you've been there, right?"

43

"Well…" Bobby hesitated. "I'm just not sure. It started out pretty cool…" "HOW ABOUT CRASHING INTO THOSE BUSHES?" Siggy demanded. "WAS THAT COOL? HUH? **HOW COOL WAS THAT?**"

Bobby considered. "I got so carried away with how cool it feels to go up, I kind of forgot about the coming down. So I've got to admit, landing in the hedge was not cool. Not cool, the hedge."

"Yeah," said Harry. "I think you're right. Cool, and then not so cool. So no more jumping over my rail, okay?"

"Okay," said Bobby. "Once was enough."

Harry nodded, and sat down next to Bobby.

"Hey! Since when is it cool to lose?" said Siggy angrily,

and he stalked off, with his friends behind him.

The servers started serving again. Kids started talking and eating.

Harry leaned over. "You know, Bobby," Harry said, so quietly that no one else could hear. "Many catch air. Only a few take flight."

"You noticed that, too?"

Harry nodded. "You got some real hang time. But the next time you try to fly that thing, I want you to come with me. I know a good spot, with a nice soft landing area . . ."

THE END